WHERE IS THUMBKIN?

Retold by STEVEN ANDERSON

Illustrated by DOREEN MARTS

CANTATA
LEARNING
MANKATO, MINNESOTA

WWW.CANTATALEARNING.COM

CANTATA LEARNING

MANKATO, MINNESOTA

Published by Cantata Learning
1710 Roe Crest Drive
North Mankato, MN 56003
www.cantatalearning.com

Library of Congress Control Number: 2014957033
978-1-63290-281-8 (hardcover/CD)
978-1-63290-433-1 (paperback/CD)
978-1-63290-475-1 (paperback)

Where is Thumbkin? by Steven Anderson
Illustrated by Doreen Marts

Book design, Tim Palin Creative
Editorial direction, Flat Sole Studio
Executive musical production and direction, Elizabeth Draper
Music arranged and produced by Steven C Music

Printed in the United States of America.

You have two hands. Each hand has five fingers.

Did you know that your fingers have names?

Now turn the page, and sing along.

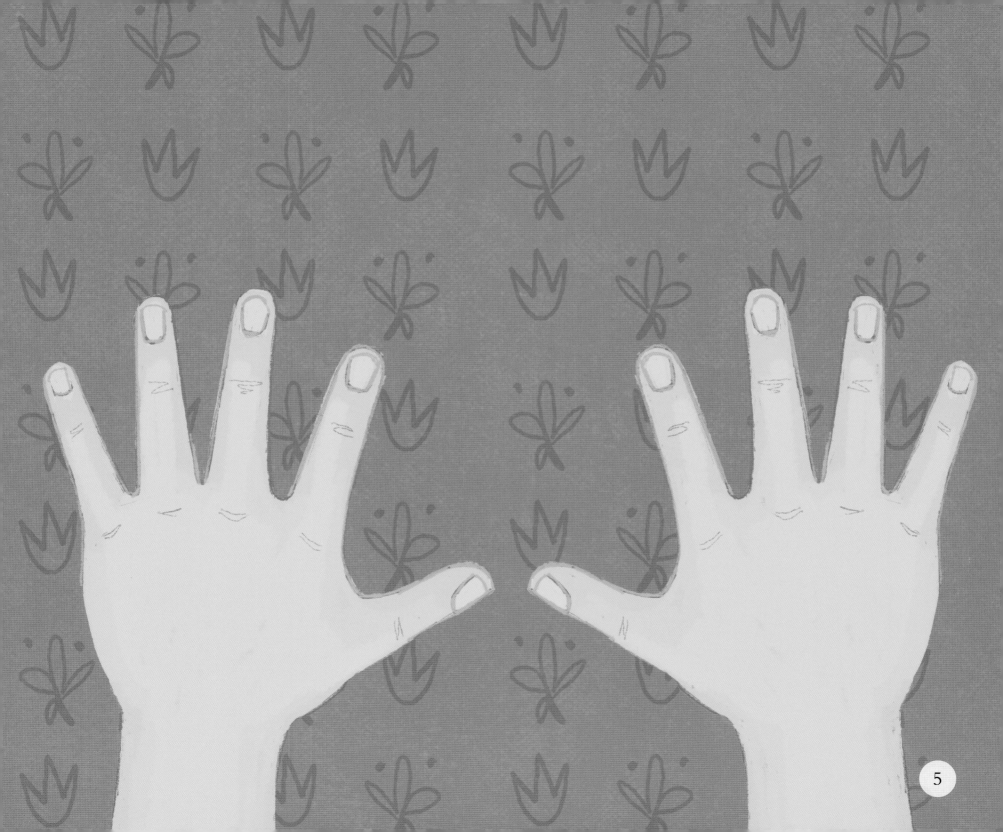

Where is Thumbkin?

Where is Thumbkin?

Here I am!

Here I am!

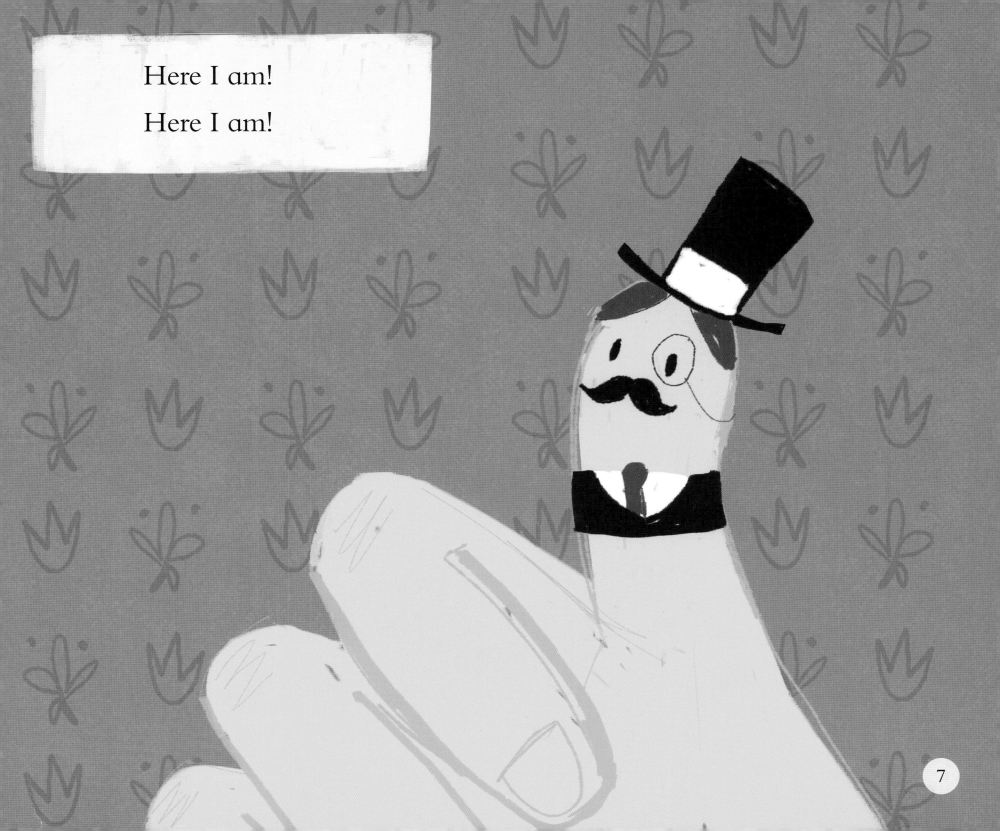

How are you today, **sir**?

Very well, I **thank** you.

Run away.

Run away.

Where is Pointer?

Where is Pointer?

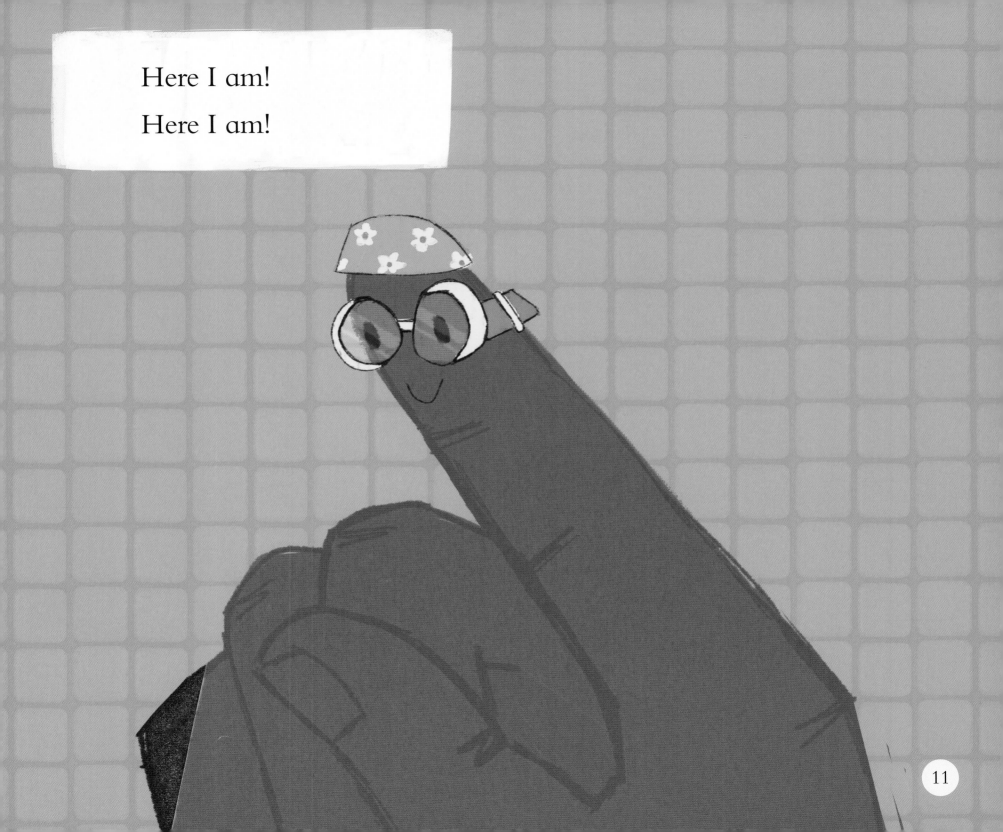

Here I am!

Here I am!

11

How are you today, sir?

Very well, I thank you.

Run away.

Run away.

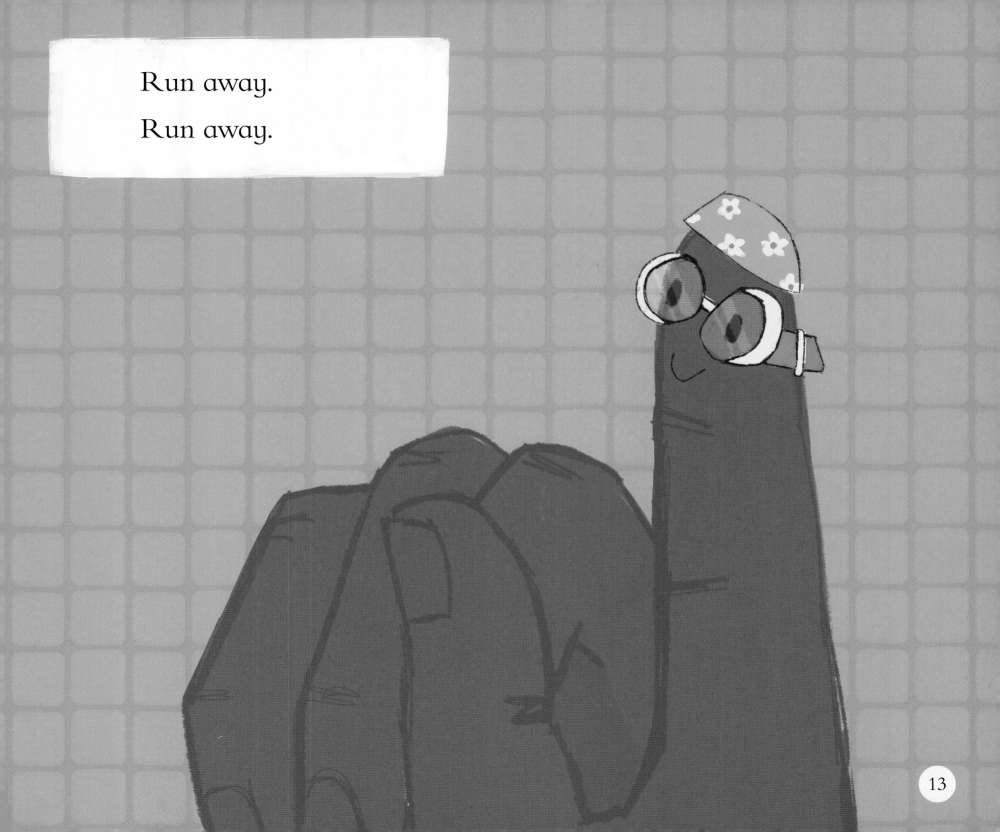

Where is Middleman?

Where is Middleman?

Here I am!

Here I am!

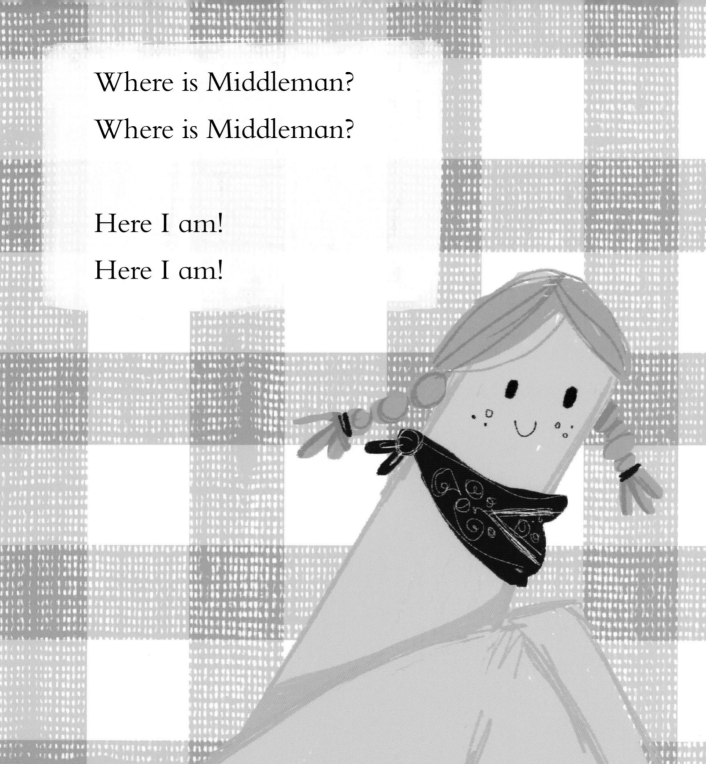

How are you today, sir?

Very well, I thank you.

Run away.

Run away.

Where is Ringman?

Where is Ringman?

Here I am!

Here I am!

How are you today, sir?
Very well, I thank you.

Run away.
Run away.

Where is Pinky?
Where is Pinky?

Here I am!
Here I am!

19

How are you today, sir?

Very well, I thank you.

Run away.

Run away.

21

SONG LYRICS
Where Is Thumbkin?

Where is Thumbkin?
Where is Thumbkin?

Here I am!
Here I am!

How are you today, sir?
Very well, I thank you.

Run away.
Run away.

Where is Pointer?
Where is Pointer?

Here I am!
Here I am!

How are you today, sir?
Very well, I thank you.

Run away.
Run away.

Where is Middleman?
Where is Middleman?

Here I am!
Here I am!

How are you today, sir?
Very well, I thank you.

Run away.
Run away.

Where is Ringman?
Where is Ringman?

Here I am!
Here I am!

How are you today, sir?
Very well, I thank you.

Run away.
Run away.

Where is Pinky?
Where is Pinky?

Here I am!
Here I am!

How are you today, sir?
Very well, I thank you.

Run away.
Run away.

Where Is Thumbkin?

Americana
Steven C Music

Verses 1-3

1. Where is Thumb-kin? Where is Thumb-kin? Here I am! Here I am!

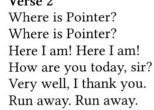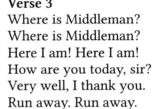

How are you to-day, sir? Ver-y well, I thank you. Run a-way. Run a-way.

Verse 2
Where is Pointer?
Where is Pointer?
Here I am! Here I am!
How are you today, sir?
Very well, I thank you.
Run away. Run away.

Verse 3
Where is Middleman?
Where is Middleman?
Here I am! Here I am!
How are you today, sir?
Very well, I thank you.
Run away. Run away.

Verses 4-5

4. Where is Ring-man? Where is Ring-man? Here I am! Here I am!

How are you to-day, sir? Ver-y well, I thank you. Run a-way. Run a-way.

Verse 5
Where is Pinky?
Where is Pinky?
Here I am! Here I am!
How are you today, sir?
Very well, I thank you.
Run away. Run away.

GLOSSARY

sir—a polite and respectful name to call a man

thank—to tell someone that you are grateful; people who are respectful thank others for favors they have done for them and for the nice things they have said to them.

GUIDED READING ACTIVITIES

1. Trace around your hand on a piece of paper. Try to label each finger. Which one is Thumbkin?

2. Look at one of the illustrations in the book. Describe to a friend or write about what is happening in the illustration.

3. Count by 5 to 20. Use your fingers if you need help.

TO LEARN MORE

Christelow, Eileen. *Five Little Monkeys Jumping on the Bed*. Boston: Clarion Books, 2014.

Collier-Morales, Roberta. *Where Is Thumbkin?* North Mankato, MN: The Child's World, 2014.

Reasoner, Charles. *This Little Piggy*. North Mankato, MN: Picture Window Books, 2013.

Rustad, Martha E. H. *My Body*. North Mankato, MN: Capstone Press, 2014.